ISBN: 9781695228344

I came to New Hampshire, in the Fall, to view the foliage. The trees are full of colored leaves. I also see the state bug, the ladybug. I wonder why it isn't the mosquito [muh-skee-toh]. I see a lot more mosquitos than ladybugs.
Hmm!

I arrive at an orchard to look for a pumpkin. The state fruit is the pumpkin, really? What do you get when you divide a pumpkin's circumference? [ser-kuhm-fer-uhns] with its diameter?
Pie! Yummy!

Birch trees are the state tree. It's a scratching post dream. Why do I prefer birch trees over dogs?
Their bark is quieter! Snicker, snicker!

I came to the White Mountains, even though they are green until the winter. I imitate the state animal, the white-tailed deer. At least something is white up here. How would I look with a white tail?
Nah!

Granite is the state rock.
I'm scratching in the
White Mountains. What a
great claw sharpener!
What do rocks eat?
Pom-a-granites!
Hee, hee!

Smokey-quartz, is the state gem, also in the White Mountains. I can't believe it's a gem. I'm going to cover it like I do with my gems in my litter box!
Ha, ha!

The state mineral is beryl [ber-uh l] and is found all over the state. I can't find anything funny about it, so I will just play with it.
Giggle!

The state sport is skiing. I ski in Sunapee [Sun-a-pee] and the White Mountains, in the winter. I steer with my tail and always wear my helmet.
Fun, fun!

I don't even know what to say about these. The lady-slipper is the state wildflower. I feel like I should cover my eyes.

In the Spring, the flowers come out. The lilac [li-lac], the state flower is my favorite color! Purrrr-ple!

The Karner-blue is the state butterfly. I can feel butterflies in my stomach!
Just kidding, I know they are endangered!

The Purple-finch, the state bird, looks pink to me! Why can't I see that bird anymore?
Because it is in da-skies! Snort!

These look fun! The red spotted newt is the state amphibian [am-phib-i-an]. Is it true they can grow back their tails?
Just joking, don't worry!

FK

In the summer I travel to the Atlantic [At-lan-tik] Ocean to find striped bass, the state salt-water fish.
Yummy!

I also visit Lake Winnipesaukee [win-uh-puh-saw-kee] to play with brook trout, the state fish.
Don't worry, I'll be nice!

I dig up some potatoes, the state vegetable. I think they must be sleeping because their eyes are closed.
Bahaha!

The state has a state dog?
The Chinook!
He looks dumb with his tongue
hanging out!
How about a state cat?

So, there is a state wildcat, the Bobcat.
I think I would be the better choice. Right?

Okay, I can be the state domestic cat. The domestic, long-hair calico.
That's me! What do you think?

LIVE FREE OR DIE
FAT KITTY
New HAMPSHIRE
9
2019

And it is okay because I live here now!

Fat Kitty

Domestic, long-hair calico for the New Hampshire State Domestic Cat.

Made in the USA
Middletown, DE
05 March 2020

85580143R00024